To Jesse, Claire, and all the ones who see differently

—R. H.

Library of Congress Cataloging-in-Publication Data:

Names: Henderson, R. (Robert Galloway), 1979- author, illustrator.
Title: I see, I see. / by R. Henderson.
Description: San Francisco, California : Chronicle Books, [2019] | Summary: This picture book of opposites encourages readers to manipulate the book, and so see things from a completely different perspective.
Identifiers: LCCN 2019001959 | ISBN 9781452183343 (alk. paper)
Subjects: LCSH: Polarity—Juvenile fiction. | Picture books for children. | Toy and movable books—Specimens. | CYAC: Stories in rhyme. | English language—Synonyms and antonyms—Fiction. | LCGFT: Toy and movable books. | Picture books.
Classification: LCC PZ8.3.H4146 Iap 2019 | DDC 823.92 [E]—dc23 LC record available at https://lccn.loc.gov/2019001959

Manufactured in China.

MIX
Paper from responsible sources
FSC™ C008047

Design by Robert Henderson and Jay Marvel.
Typeset in Henderson Slab and Brandon Grotesque.
The illustrations in this book were digitally rendered.

10 9 8 7 6 5 4 3 2 1

Chronicle Books LLC
680 Second Street
San Francisco, California 94107

I See, I See.

by R. Henderson

chronicle books · san francisco

How to read together!

1. Readers face each other across the book.
2. Reader marked ★ reads first.
3. Second reader responds.

. . . I see last.

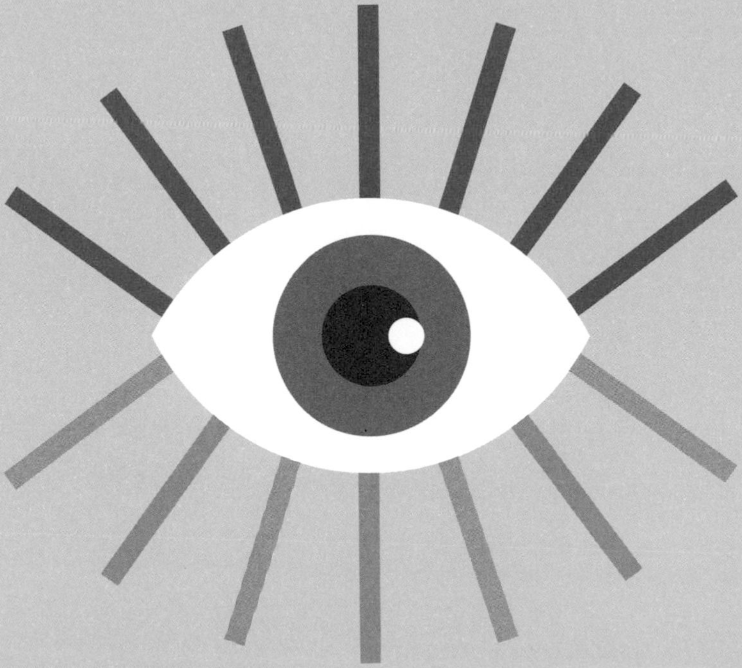

I see first page . . .

. . . I see past.

I see future . . .

I see up . . .

. . . and I see down.

I see smile . . .

. . . and I see frown.

. . . I see sky.

★ I see water . . .

I see swim . . .

. . . and I see fly.

Left ways,
right ways,
upside down.

Take the book
and spin it 'round.

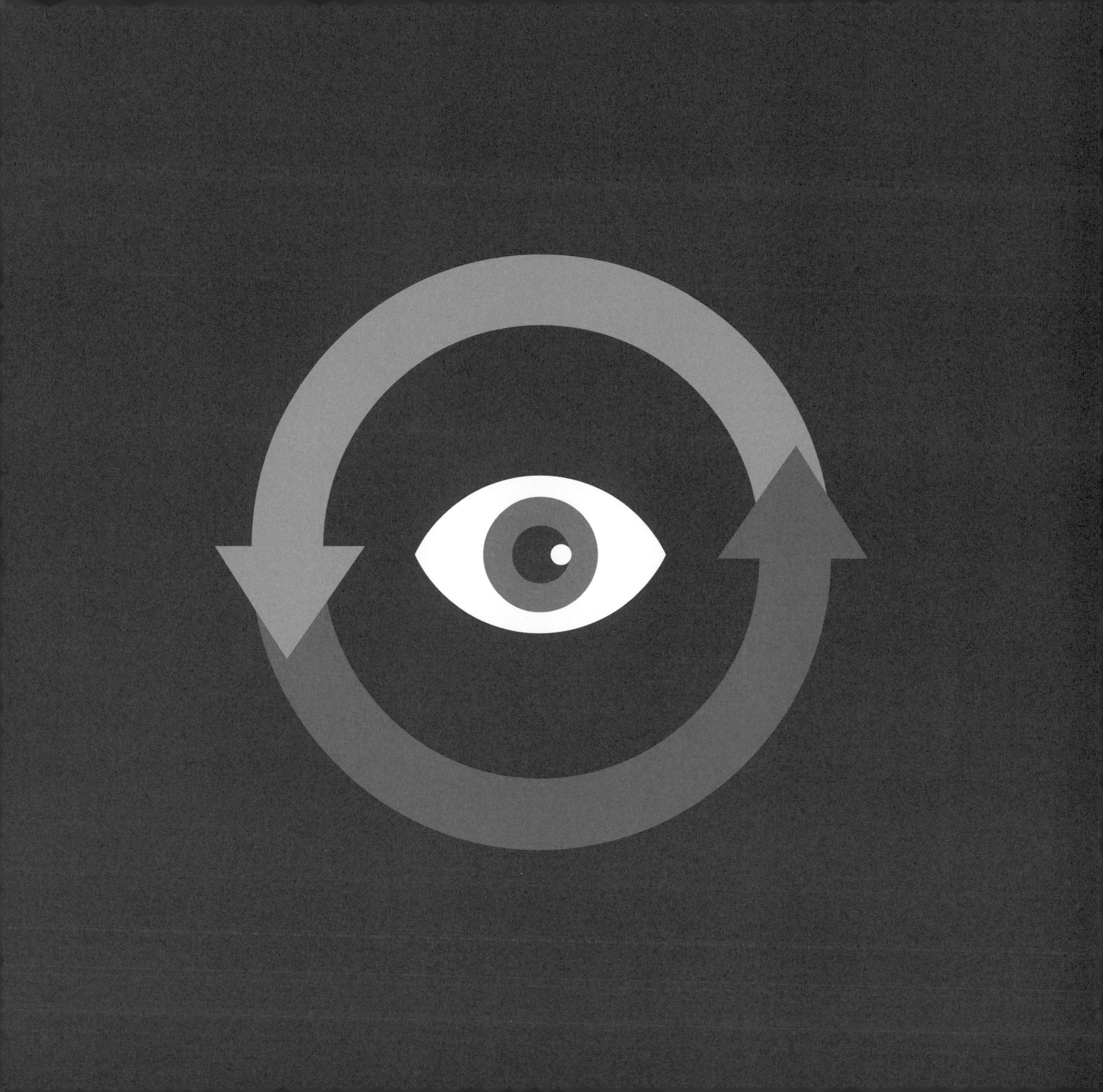

I see empty . . .

. . . I see full.

I see push . . .

. . . and I see pull.

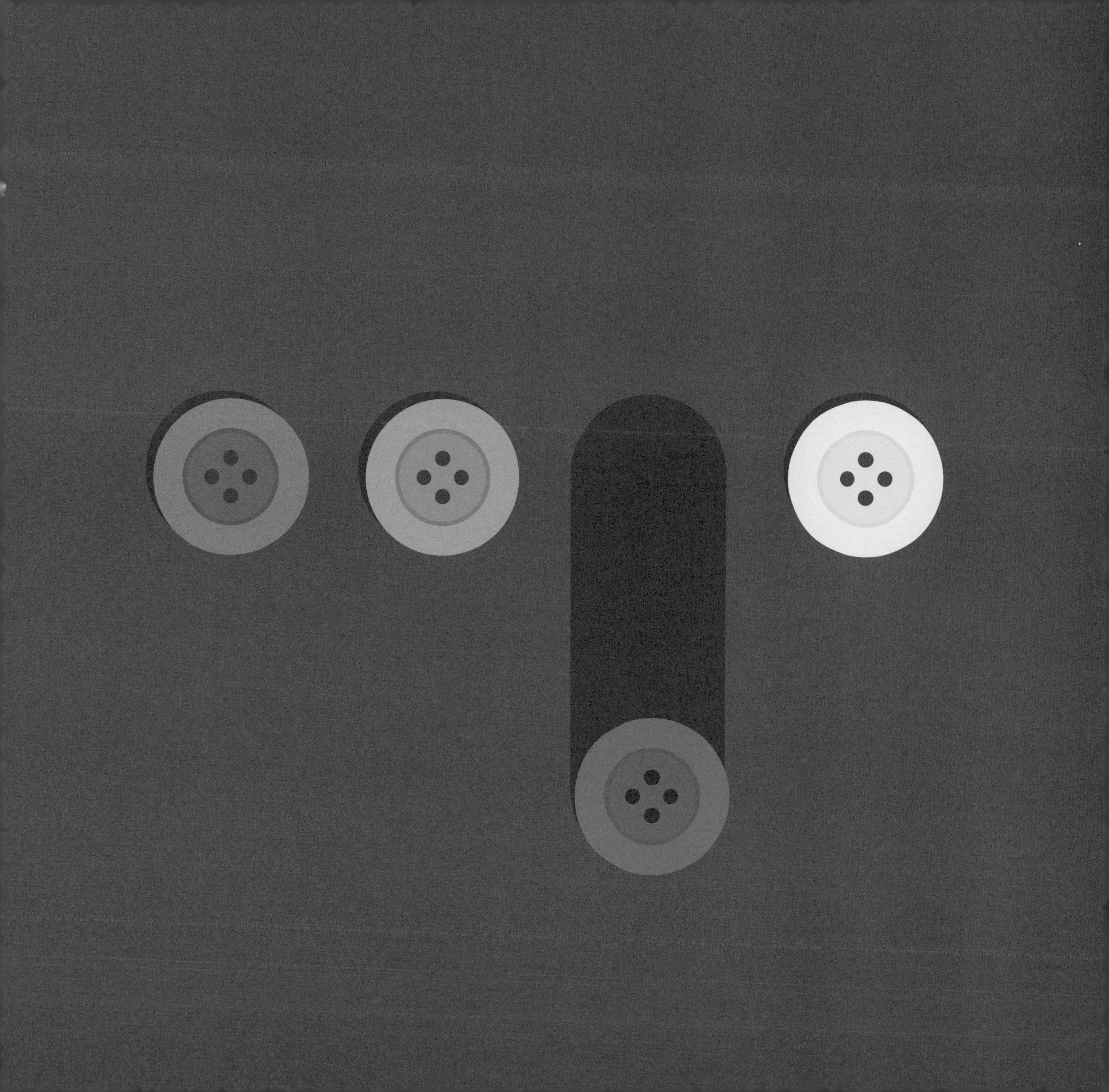

I see left . . .

. . . and I see right.

I see day . . .

. . . and I see night.

I see yuck . . .

. . . and I see yum.

I see dad . . .

. . . and I see mum.

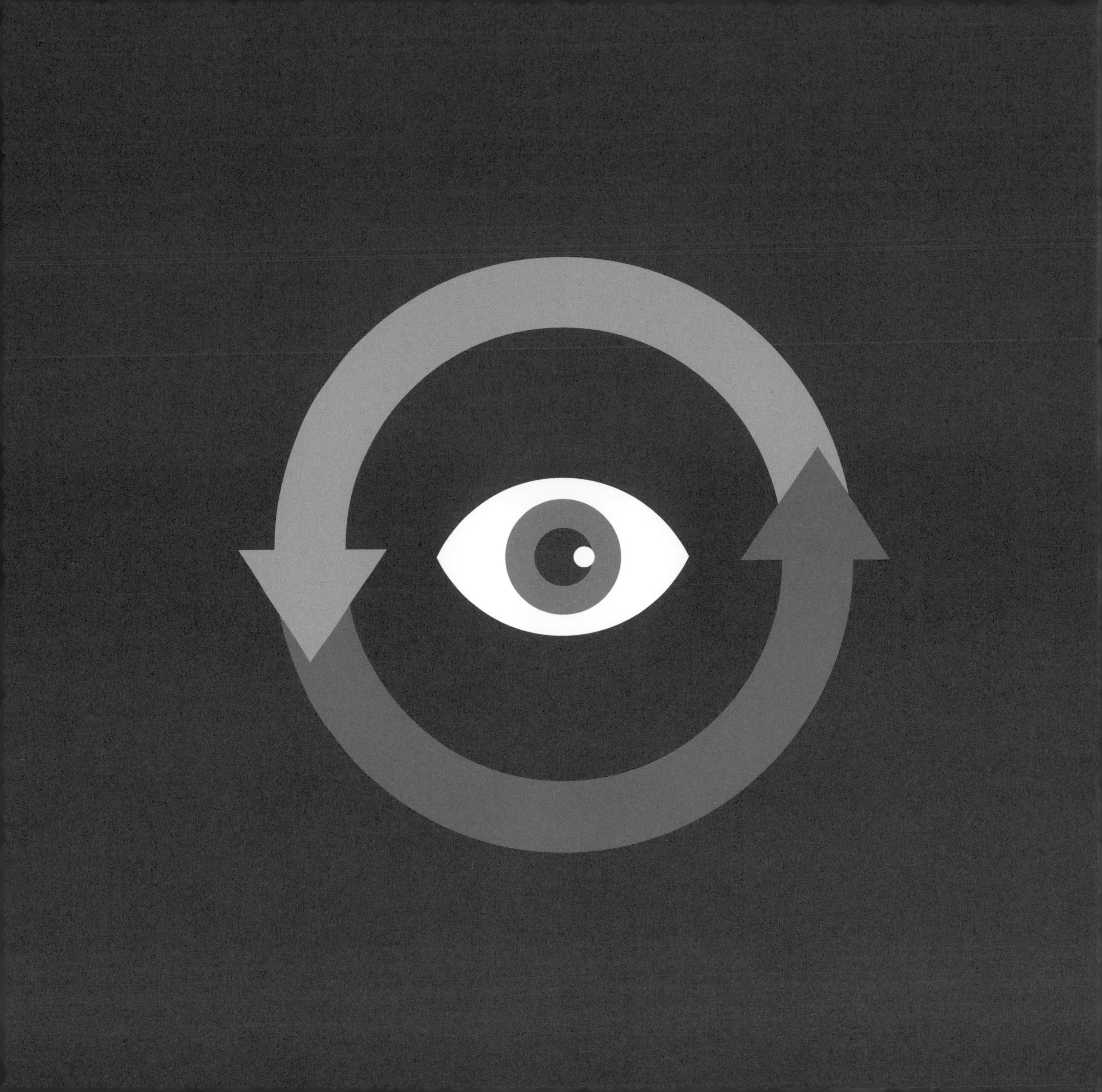

High or low
or day or night.

Turn the book
to see who's right.

★ I see two peaks . . .

. . . I see three.

. . . I see tree.

★ I see forest . . .

★ I see high . . .

. . . and I see low.

I see stop . . .

. . . and I see go.

I see best . . .

. . . and I see worst.

. . . I see first.

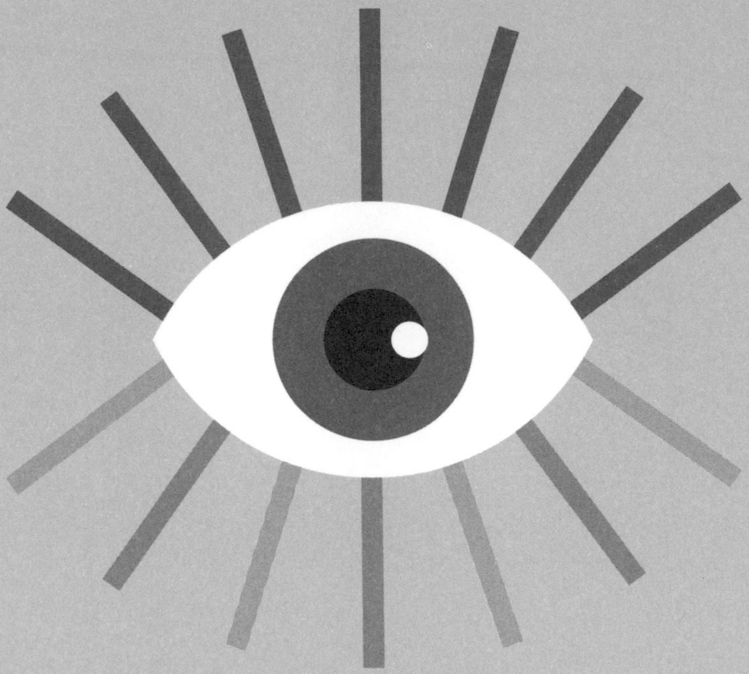

I see last page . . .

R. Henderson is a prolific non-graduate from a range of prestigious Australian universities and an actual graduate of Griffith University's Queensland College of Art. Robert lives in Brisbane with his partner and two young children who help him with his work and make sure he never has to eat a sandwich by himself.